For Chloë and Theo
—M. F.

For my grandson, Blue, with love
—J. D.

A Note from the Illustrator

The polar bears in this book were made by needle felting, which is a process of stabbing wool
with a barbed needle in order to change the density of the fibers. I began with a wire armature,
wrapped my wool around it, continuously "stabbing," while I added more wool in order to sculpt
each bear. The polar bear house was made with chicken wire and papier mâché covered in velvet.
Jeanne Birdsall and I set up the scenes, and she photographed them.

BEACH LANE BOOKS
An imprint of Simon & Schuster Children's Publishing Division
1230 Avenue of the Americas, New York, New York 10020
Text copyright © 2019 by Mem Fox
Illustrations copyright © 2019 by Jane Dyer
Photography by Jeanne Birdsall
All rights reserved, including the right of reproduction in whole or in part in any form.
BEACH LANE BOOKS is a trademark of Simon & Schuster, Inc.
For information about special discounts for bulk purchases, please contact Simon & Schuster Special Sales at 1-866-506-1949 or
business@simonandschuster.com.
The Simon & Schuster Speakers Bureau can bring authors to your live event. For more information or to book an event,
contact the Simon & Schuster Speakers Bureau at 1-866-248-3049 or visit our website at www.simonspeakers.com.
Book design by Sonia Chaghatzbanian
The text for this book was set in Aldus.
Manufactured in China
0819 SCP
First Edition
10 9 8 7 6 5 4 3 2 1
Library of Congress Cataloging-in-Publication Data
Names: Fox, Mem, 1946– author. | Dyer, Jane, illustrator.
Title: Roly Poly / Mem Fox ; illustrated by Jane Dyer.
Description: First edition. | New York : Beach Lane Books, [2019] | Summary: Roly Poly the polar bear never wanted a brother,
but then little Monty arrives and Roly Poly has to adjust to his new sibling.
Identifiers: LCCN 2018045183 | ISBN 9781481445566 (hardcover : alk. paper) | ISBN 9781481445573 (eBook : alk. paper)
Subjects: | CYAC: Brothers—Fiction. | Polar bear—Fiction. | Bears—Fiction.
Classification: LCC PZ7.F8373 Ro 2019 | DDC [E]—dc23 LC record available at https://lccn.loc.gov/2018045183

Roly Poly

Mem Fox • Jane Dyer

Beach Lane Books

New York London Toronto Sydney New Delhi

Once upon a time, way up near the top of the world, there lived a polar bear named Roly Poly. He had a father and a mother, but no sister or brother.

The bed he slept in
was his bed, and his alone.

The fish he caught were his fish,
and his alone.

The walrus tooth he played
with was his walrus tooth,
and his alone.

Life was grand.

Then one morning, Roly Poly found a perfect stranger sharing his very own bed.

"Who is *that*?" he asked.

"A little brother," said his father.

"His name is Monty."

"A little brother?" said Roly Poly.
"But I never asked for a little brother, and
 I don't want one now."

"I know," said his mother.
"But we think you will
adore him."

Roly Poly put his nose in the air and pretended not to hear.

Monty tumbled all over him.
"Hey," said Roly Poly. "Don't *do* that!
I never asked for a little brother, and
I don't want one now."

He stood up and stormed off.

Later, Monty sat on him.
"Hey," said Roly Poly. "Don't *do* that! I never asked for a little brother, and I don't want one now."

He stood up and stormed off again.

"I'm coming too," said Monty.
Roly Poly put his nose in the
air and pretended not to hear.

A little later, Roly Poly caught a fish.

He was just about to eat that fish
when Monty grabbed it from him.

"Hey," said Roly Poly. "Don't *do* that! I never asked for a little brother, and I *certainly* don't want one now."

He stormed off again, clutching the walrus tooth tightly to his chest.

"I'm coming too," said Monty.

Roly Poly put his nose in the air and pretended not to hear.

Monty crept up behind Roly Poly and snatched the walrus tooth right out of his paws.

"Get lost!" yelled Roly Poly.
"Get lost right *now*!"

At precisely that moment,
the ice beneath them
groaned, and . . .

cracked, and broke in two.

Monty began to drift away.

Roly Poly put his nose in the air
and pretended not to notice.

The gap in the ice grew wider.
"Help!" cried Monty. "Help!"
Roly Poly pretended not to hear.

"HELP!" cried Monty again.

At which point, Roly Poly could bear it no longer.
"Don't cry, little Monty!" he called out.
"Please don't cry. I'm on my way."

And he leapt into the icy sea.

From that day onward, believe it or not and in spite of everything, Roly Poly and his little brother lived happily ever after.

Well. . . .

Mostly.